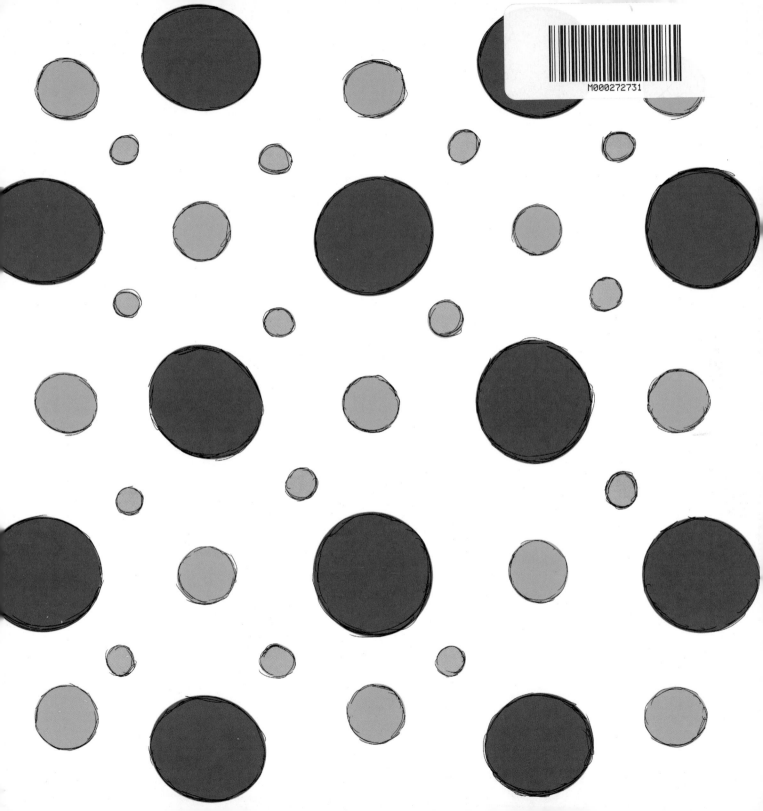

This book is dedicated to my sweet husband and awesome kids. Thank you for pushing me through my own self doubt and for loving me during the times that my own anxiety monster gets a little too big and wild.

A big thank you to my little artist helpers for their monster designs: Jack age 7, Alex age 11, and Jane age 7

INSPIRE JOY PUBLISHING, LLC
TEXT AND ILLUSTRATION COPYRIGHT © 2020 BY MELANIE HAWKINS
FIRST EDITION

Paperback Edition: ISBN 978-1-7341650-8-1
Hardback Edition: ISBN 978-1-7341650-9-8
Library of Congress Control Number: 2020910002

Ispire Joy Publishing can provide special discounts when purchased in larger volumes for premiums and Promotional purpose, as well as for fundraising and educational use.

Contact: MelanieHawkinsAuthor@gmail.com   https://melaniehawkinsauthor.wordpress.com/
https://www.facebook.com/inspirejoypublishing   Instagram.com/melaniehawkinsauthor

My Anxiety Monster

I am stronger than my anxiety!
I am in control! I can make a plan!
I can talk it out with someone that understands!
I know how to do hard things! I can get through this!
My anxiety is only a small part of who I am!
My anxiety does not define me!

By:_____

How to Tame My Anxiety Monster

Written and Illustrated
by Melanie Hawkins

Do you want to know a secret?

There's a monster that likes to visit me that only I can see.

Sometimes he feels big and scary.

Sometimes he likes to visit me when I'm scared, or worried, or sometimes when I'm happy or just playing.

I don't always like when he visits me.

Sometimes he feels big and scary.
Sometimes he makes me feel tired and
it's hard to concentrate.

Sometimes it is
hard to sleep.

I feel restless when he's around and
often feel angry.

Sometimes my heart beats faster, and I might start shaking, sweating, or my tummy may hurt.

I might also feel dizzy, too, or like I can't breathe.

I don't like this at all.

I decided to talk to my parents about it. I thought they wouldn't believe me.

But they did!

Mom has a monster that visits her, too. Her monster is just like mine.

She told me some things about her monster. Our monsters are very similar.

He really is a good monster to have around. He wants to be helpful, but he's big and gets excited easily.

He doesn't always know how to behave, just like a new puppy. I just need to learn to train him.

When I talk about my monster to someone else that understands, it feels good.

There are some tricks that I can teach him so that he will learn to behave.

Do you want to know my monster's name?
His name is Anxiety.
Giving him a name makes him not quite so scary.
It's like naming a new pet.

Learning more about him helps me understand
him and why he likes to visit me so much.

I am brave, and strong, and can train him even when he might seem big or scary.

I do feel brave!

Here are some things I can do to train my monster.

When I get outside to play, go on a walk, or exercise it can give me special super boosters called endorphins. It makes him a happy monster that can be helpful to me with sports or other activities.

When I do yoga, breathe deeply,
and clear my mind from worries it
can help him shrink.

That's kind of
neat!

When I do art, it calms me and can help me see that he's not so big and not quite so scary...I don't think he looks so scary now!

When my monster gets a little too big and wild, having a plan helps me stay in control.

He likes to be helpful, but sometimes he gets a little too big and wild. He doesn't always know how to behave.

Planning what to do if he acts up can help me tame him.

It's helpful to know that lots of people have an anxiety monster that likes to visit them, too...

my aunt,

my neighbor,

and my friend.

When he is really bothering me, remembering my five senses helps to keep me in control.

I can look at something that  makes me happy.

 I can smell something nice.

I can touch something that has texture.

I can listen to something that makes me feel peaceful.

I can taste something delicious.

All of these tricks take my focus off of my monster, which can calm him down.

If I need a little extra help learning how to train him, there are special doctors or counselors that can help me.

My monster likes to visit me because I
have a very big, kind, caring heart that
feels emotions very deeply...

and that is a really good thing!

He really does want me to feel all of my special feelings

without being afraid!

He can be really helpful when I'm playing sports or if I have to talk in front of the class.

Book
Reports
Today

He can even be helpful if I have a big test to study for.

He loves to do scary-fun things
with me like go for a ride on a...

ROLLERCOASTER!

I am stronger than my monster.
Even with him around, I can still do all of the
things I need to do.

I don't think he'll be a
problem anymore.

But if he is, I know how to tame my anxiety monster!

The
End

Talking points for parents, teachers, and helpers:
What is Anxiety?

Anxiety is the body and mind's natural way of dealing with fear or worry. It can make children irritable and angry, and even cause sleeping troubles. It can also cause physical symptoms like headaches, fatigue, or stomachaches. Sometimes children with anxiety may keep it hidden, making the symptoms easily missed. It is important to talk with a professional if you suspect anxiety in you or your child.

What are the signs of anxiety in children?

Anxiety can make you feel scared, panicky, or embarrassed.
Some of the signs to look out for are:
* Difficulty concentrating
* Restlessness or waking up in the night with bad dreams
* Not eating properly, feeling a "lump" in the throat, or difficulty swallowing.
* Often feeling angry or irritable, or having outbursts and feeling out of control
* Excessive worrying, especially about things you cannot control
* Feeling tense and fidgety, picking at skin, nails, or hair
* Excessive crying or feeling sad
* Being clingy all the time when other children seem to be okay
* Complaining of tummy aches and not feeling well
You might not even recognize why you're feeling this way. Anxiety can look different depending on the age or situation. Younger children might have separation anxiety, where older children may tend to worry more about tests, friends, tryouts, etc.
It is important to always speak to a doctor to get a diagnosis if you suspect anxiety.

Tools that can help:

1. Learn about your anxiety, what it is, and what triggers it for you. (This may change over time or with different situations).
2. Exercise regularly. Getting regular aerobic exercise has been shown to decrease tension, stabilize mood, and help you sleep better.
3. Try meditation. It can help quiet your brain and teach you how to turn off the constant cycle of worry.
4. Art or having another creative outlet can help you feel a sense of calm as you become more self aware and can give you a much needed emotional release.
5. Having a plan in place can help ease anxiety of the unknown, but it can also help to be prepared for known anxiety-inducing triggers.
6. Talking about your anxiety is helpful. Make feelings heard and validated by NOT saying things like: that's silly, or it's all in your head, or just get over it, or don't worry.
7. Use your five senses during an anxiety attack: sight, smell, touch, hearing, and taste. This can help ground you with things that you do have control over.
8. Always reach out to a doctor, counselor, therapist, or psychologist who can give you guidance and help put together a treatment plan if needed.

Little Artists Submissions:

Jane 7   Declan 9   Jude 8   Trishelle 8   Annelise 8   Tanaaya 6   Claire 7

Alex 11   Jesse 11   Jack 7   Jules 5   Tanner 10   Jonah 10

Meet the Author & Illustrator

Author and illustrator Melanie Hawkins was born and raised in the United States in a charming little farming town in Idaho, but has made her home in the beautiful state of Utah. She and her wonderful husband have 7 amazing children. Her family is her greatest source of joy and inspiration. She is an Elementary Art Teacher and enjoys camping, swimming, dark chocolate, and movie nights with her family. In her spare time she can be found painting, sewing, writing, and illustrating children's books. She is an eternal optimist and wishes that everyone could see the world as she does with all of its beauty, hope, and goodness. This book was a truly inspired work of heart for her. She hopes it will help others that struggle with taming their Anxiety monsters as well!

Books by Author and Illustrator
Melanie Hawkins
(with more coming soon)

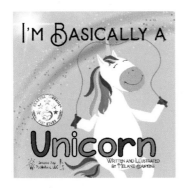

I'm Basically a
Unicorn

Little Bug and
the Noisy New
Neighbor

Little Bug and
the Christmas
Surprise

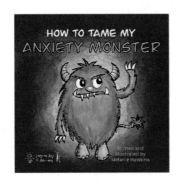

How To Tame
My Anxiety
Monster

Connect:

Email: MelanieHawkinsAuthor@gmail.com

Facebook: @inspirejoypublishing

Instagram: @melaniehawkinsauthor

https://www.amazon.com/Melanie-Hawkins/
e/B07ZXWN84P/

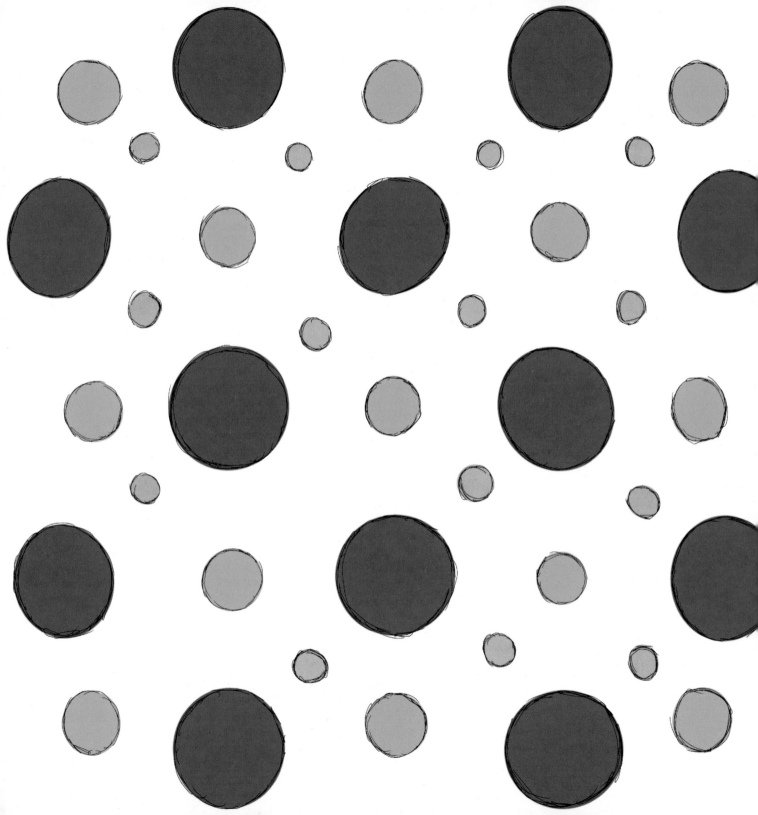

Made in the USA
Monee, IL
24 April 2022

95330122R00024

DO YOU HAVE AN Anxiety Monster?

Is there any way to tame him? Can he be a helpful Monster that you may not mind having around?

Find out in this delightful new book with practical solutions just for kids that deal with anxiety!

ISBN 978-1-7341650-8-1   US$12.99

9 781734 165081   51299